Blue
Chameleon

Emily Gravett

Simon & Schuster Books for Young Readers

NEW YORK   LONDON   TORONTO   SYDNEY

Blue chameleon

Yellow

banana

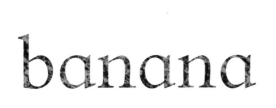

Pink

cockatoo

Swirly

snail

Brown

boot

Stripy

sock

ball

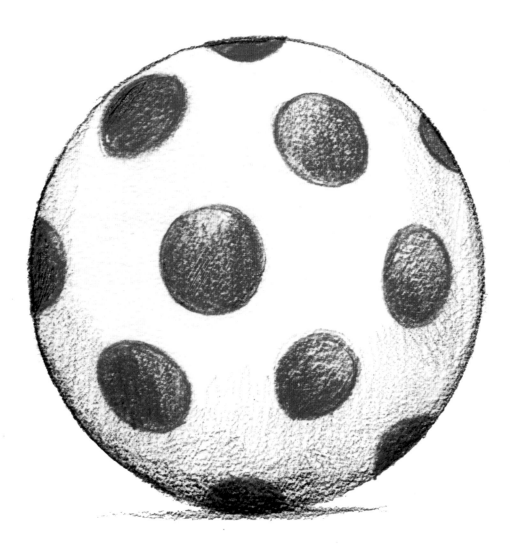

Gold

fish

Green
grasshopper

Gray

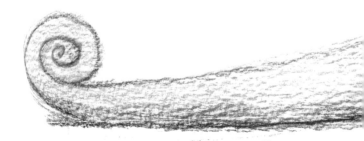

rock

White

page

Hello?

Colorful

chameleons